# YOU NOTICE A LIGHT IN ONE OF THE CASTLE WINDOWS AND BEGIN TO WALK TOWARD IT . . .

You are shivering from the cold. The sky is still dark and stormy, and great streaks of lightning light up the night.

During one long flash of lightning, you discover that you are walking through a cemetery. You see shapes moving in the darkness and wonder if your own fear is creating an illusion . . . or if there really are spirits floating around you.

Your fear increases when you step on a rock, and a tombstone moves to reveal a door in the ground.

*If you choose to go through the door and into the tunnel below, turn to page 23.*

*If you prefer to investigate the light in the castle, turn to page 24.*

**REMEMBER, YOU ARE MASTER OF YOUR OWN FATE!**

**WHICH WAY BOOKS** for you to enjoy

Available from ARCHWAY paperbacks

Most Archway Paperbacks are available at special quantity discounts
for bulk purchases for sales promotions, premiums or fund raising.
Special books or book excerpts can also be created to fit specific needs.

For details write the office of the Vice President of Special Markets,
Pocket Books, 1230 Avenue of the Americas, New York, New York
10020.

WHICH WAY BOOKS #1

# THE CASTLE OF NO RETURN

## R.G. Austin

### ILLUSTRATED BY MIKE EAGLE

**AN ARCHWAY PAPERBACK**
Published by POCKET BOOKS • NEW YORK

AN ARCHWAY PAPERBACK *Original*

An Archway Paperback published by
POCKET BOOKS, a Simon & Schuster division of
GULF & WESTERN CORPORATION
1230 Avenue of the Americas, New York, N.Y. 10020

ISBN: 0-671-47372-7

First Archway Paperback printing January, 1982

10  9  8  7  6  5

For Ben, with love
and thanks for all his help

# THE CASTLE OF NO RETURN

# Attention!

*Which Way Books* must be read in a special way. DO NOT READ THE PAGES IN ORDER. If you do, the story will make no sense at all. Instead, follow the directions at the bottom of each page until you come to an ending. Only then should you return to the beginning and start over again, making different choices this time.

There are many possibilities for exciting adventures. Some of the endings are good; some of the endings are bad. If you meet a terrible fate, you can reverse it in your next story by making new choices.

Remember: follow the directions carefully and have fun!

One night as you are watching your favorite television program, the picture begins to wiggle, and a loud buzz fills the room. You try to adjust the set, but nothing works. In fact, the picture gets worse, and the buzz gets louder. Angry and frustrated, you turn off the TV.

You talk to your friends and discover that every television set in town has been disrupted.

The next morning you hear strange electronic sounds. You discover that they are coming from the woods behind your house, and you decide to investigate them.

You put your Swiss Army knife into your pocket and set out in the direction of the noise.

*(continued on page 3)*

You have been hiking for hours when the sky suddenly turns black, and you are caught in a fierce storm.

The storm is short, but you are wet and shivering when you come to a part of the woods that you have never seen before.

In front of you is a castle—a real castle, with a moat and turrets and high walls.

To the side of you is a rickety old shack.

*If you choose to swim the moat in order to reach the castle, turn to page 4.*

*If you want to explore the shack, turn to page 5.*

Just as you are about to dive into the moat, a drawbridge is lowered in front of you. Its cranking and creaking sounds are eerie, and there is a loud thud as the bridge hits the ground.

You cross to the other side and enter the courtyard through a door in the wall. As you step into the courtyard, the bridge lifts. Your exit has been closed.

You look around and discover a bright beam of light. You are ready to investigate the light when you hear a piercing scream.

*If you want to help the person who screamed, turn to page 8.*

*If you decide to investigate the beam of light, turn to page 9.*

You walk toward the shack. There is no light inside, but you hope that the door is unlocked so that you can go in and warm yourself.

By now you are shivering so violently that

*(continued on page 6)*

your whole body is shaking. You can barely control yourself enough to knock on the door.

Just as you raise your hand, you hear the ferocious growl of a dog.

*If you decide to knock on the door and enter the shack, turn to page 7.*

*If you decide that you do not want to go in, turn to page 10.*

You knock. A light goes on, and the door opens slowly.

"Hello," says a man. "My name is Boris. Please come in from the cold."

You glance at the huge mastiff that is chained to the wall.

"Do not worry about Killer," says Boris. "He will not do anything without my command."

"All right," you say in a shaking voice as you enter the shack.

"You look hungry," Boris says. "Would you like a bowl of soup?"

*If you decide to eat Boris's soup, turn to page 15.*

*If you decide not to eat Boris's soup, turn to page 17.*

You have made a difficult decision: you must try to help the person who screamed.

You listen. Once more a scream echoes off the walls, but you cannot figure out where it is coming from.

Suddenly there is only silence surrounding you. You do not know where to go.

*If you decide to enter the castle, turn to page 11.*

*If you decide to explore outside the castle, turn to page 12.*

You begin to walk toward the strange beam. The light looks as if it might warm you. But when you reach it, you wonder if it might be dangerous.

Behind the light you notice a door.

*If you decide to open the door, turn to page 11.*

*If you decide to stand in the light and warm your body, turn to page 14.*

You turn to go, but you cannot leave. It is as if you are being held there by a powerful magnet.

Suddenly a light goes on, and a large bearded man opens the door. His dog, an enormous brown mastiff, is chained to the wall.

"Come in," says the man. "My name is Boris. What brings you here?"

"I...I'm looking for the source of the interference on my TV," you answer as you step inside.

"I see," says Boris. "You're very clever. You've come to the right place. There are many experiments going on here. Electronic ones that could cause trouble with your TV reception."

You do not like Boris and want to leave this place as quickly as you can.

"Well," you say. "Thank you for the information. That's all I wanted to know. I'll be going now."

You walk to the door. But right in front of your eyes, the bolt snaps shut . . . without anyone touching it.

*If you decide to stay in the shack, turn to page 18.*

*If you decide to try opening the bolt, turn to page 20.*

You approach the huge castle door. It is made of massive planks of wood with iron hinges. You are suprised at how easily it opens.

You step into an enormous entry hall.

You call out, "Hello. Is anybody there?" Your voice echoes back to you from all directions.

*If you go up the stairs that are directly in front of you, turn to page 21.*

*If you would rather see what is behind the door on your right, turn to page 22.*

You notice a light in one of the castle windows and begin to walk toward it.

You are shivering from the cold. The sky is still dark and stormy, and great streaks of lightning light up the night.

During one long flash of lightning, you discover that you are walking through a cemetery.

*(continued on page 13)*

You see shapes moving in the darkness and wonder if your own fear is creating an illusion . . . or if there really are spirits floating around you.

Your fear increases when you step on a rock, and a tombstone moves to reveal a door in the ground.

*If you choose to go through the door and into the tunnel below, turn to page 23.*

*If you prefer to investigate the light in the castle, turn to page 24.*

You stand in this strange beam of light and are grateful for the warmth. Suddenly you feel numb. A tingling sensation begins to spread over your body.

Looking down at your feet, you are horrified to discover that you are disappearing. You are filled with terror as your entire body dematerializes.

You do not know how much time has elapsed when you feel the process begin to reverse.

Stunned, you hear a strange voice say, "Welcome."

*You have no choice. Turn to page 25.*

The soup is hot and tasty, and you finish it quickly.

"I was surprised," you say, "to see a castle here in the woods. Nobody in town knows it is here."

"It has always been a secret," Boris explains. "We are involved in scientific research and do not want to be disturbed."

"What kind of research?" you ask.

"Oh, powers of the mind mostly," answers Boris. "ESP, hypnosis, psychokinesis . . . that sort of thing."

"Psycho what?" you ask, not understanding the word.

"Psychokinesis," he repeats. "The science of moving objects with the power of the mind. Watch."

Boris picks up a spoon and places it on the palm of your hand. Then he stares at the spoon

*(continued on page 16)*

with an intense, powerful glare. You feel the spoon getting warm; then it begins to twist. When Boris is finished, the spoon looks like a pretzel.

"I carry on my experiments in the Control Room," says Boris. "Would you like to see it?"

*If you want to go to the Control Room with Boris, turn to page 27.*

*If you do not want to go to the Control Room, turn to page 29.*

You refuse Boris's offer of soup as politely as you can. You sense that he is annoyed, but you do not care.

Boris begins to speak to you.

"You are sleepy . . . very sleepy," he says. "Your eyelids are heavy . . . You are very sleepy . . . You can barely keep your eyes open. . . ."

You realize that Boris is trying to hypnotize you and that you should fight off his attempt. But you are so tired that you want more than anything to close your eyes and sleep.

*If you try to resist the hypnosis, turn to page 30.*

*If you are so tired that you cannot resist, turn to page 31.*

You turn from the door and look at Boris.

"How did that happen?" you ask. "Who moved the bolt?"

"I did," Boris says. "I can move objects with my mind. I have the power of psychokinesis. Watch the table."

You watch as a spoon moves to the side of the table and drops over the edge. Then a book falls off a shelf. A pot clatters to the floor.

*(continued on page 19)*

"I do other mind experiments in my Control Room," he says. "Would you like to see it?"

You are so frightened that you cannot speak. All you can do is nod or shake your head.

*If you nod your head to indicate* yes, *turn to page 27.*

*If you shake your head to indicate* no, *turn to page 32.*

You fling open the bolt and race into the darkness. Ahead of you there are some bushes. You dash into them, hoping to hide.

You can hear Boris behind you. His footsteps are getting closer. You suddenly realize that you are in a maze of high thorny bushes.

"You are trapped," Boris calls from somewhere behind you. "No matter which way you turn, you will find a dead end."

You come to a fork in the maze.

*If you go to the right, turn to page 33.*

*If you go to the left, turn to page 34.*

You walk slowly up the long, wide flight of stairs. Just as you reach the top, you hear a scream. It is coming from the room straight ahead of you.

Your heart races. You are terrified.

Suddenly you hear pounding on the inside of the door on your right.

*If you go to the room where you heard the scream, turn to page 35.*

*If you run away down the hall, turn to page 36.*

*If you open the door on your right, turn to page 86.*

You slip inside the door, and it slams shut. You reach for the doorknob, but there is none. You are locked inside.

There is a flight of stone steps in front of you. It is very dark at the bottom.

You walk down carefully, but not carefully enough. Halfway down the stairs, you trip and fall helplessly to the bottom.

As you fall, you hit your head hard on a stone step and are knocked unconscious.

When you wake up, you are groggy and weak.

*If you want to lie there and rest for a while, turn to page 37.*

*If you choose to go on, turn to page 38.*

You descend into the tunnel. It is dark, and the walls feel damp and slimy as you touch them with your hands.

You walk through a huge, sticky spider web. It covers your face.

You are trembling with fear, but you continue your way down the tunnel until you come to a fork.

*If you go to the right, turn to page 39.*

*If you go to the left, turn to page 40.*

You climb the vine that leads to the lighted window, and you look inside.

You see that the room is some kind of biology laboratory. There are plants and animals everywhere.

Suddenly, out of nowhere, a white dove flies over to you and lands on your shoulder. You suspect that this is not an ordinary dove.

*If you decide to climb through the window and enter the laboratory, turn to page 41.*

*If you think that the dove might be trying to tell you something and that you should follow the bird, turn to page 42.*

You have rematerialized in a room inside the castle. The room is filled with caged animals and green plants.

One entire wall is a giant computer. A man and woman are in the room. The man is standing next to you, smiling.

*(continued on page 26)*

You do not like this room, although you cannot figure out why. For some reason it is threatening.

*If you try to make a run for it, turn to page 43.*

*If you decide to stay and find out what the scientists are doing, turn to page 44.*

Boris looks at you and snaps his fingers.

"Let's be off," he says as he raises a trap-door in the floor. "This way, please."

You follow him into a tunnel. As you walk, you hear the noise of animals scurrying along the path in front of you.

When you emerge from the tunnel, you realize that you are inside the castle. You follow Boris into a room that is filled with flashing lights.

You are very frightened and think that you should run from here as quickly as possible.

"That would not be wise," Boris says, reading your mind.

*If you decide to make a run for it, turn to page 47.*

*If you decide to stay and find out what happens next, turn to page 48.*

"The idea of someone else having control over my mind scares me," you tell Boris. "I'd rather not visit the Control Room. Thank you."

You think to yourself that you must find a way to escape.

"I wouldn't do that," Boris says.

"Do what?" you ask.

"Try to escape." Boris smiles. "You see? Even if we don't go to the Control Room, I can read your mind."

You move toward the window. The huge mastiff is chained right there, and he growls menacingly.

*If you try to make a run for it, turn to page 49.*

*If you decide to stay, turn to page 50.*

You are determined not to let Boris hypnotize you. You concentrate on staying awake. You think about your room at home and make a mental list of as many things in it that you can remember. You think about your cat and about pizza, about ice cream and football games. You think about Superman and Miss Piggy, rollerskating and TV.

Convinced that he has hypnotized you, Boris stops talking and prepares to go to bed. Soon he is asleep.

But you are wide awake.

*Turn to page 51.*

You become more and more woozy and are amazed at how relaxed you feel. It is almost as though you are asleep and awake at the same time. You are aware of everything that is happening in the room. The dog's growling and Boris's soothing voice sound clear but distant.

It is so pleasant, you are not even aware that you have been hypnotized.

*Turn to page 27.*

When you are finally able to speak, you tell him that you appreciate his invitation, but that you want to go home.

"You cannot leave here without my permission," says Boris. "You will go home when I tell you. Not before."

Suddenly you realize that you are a prisoner.

You look around the room to see if you can find a way out. You notice a square of wood in the center of the floor that is darker than the wood around it. Then you see a small metal ring in the center of the square. You suspect that it is a trapdoor.

You also notice a heavy jug on the table.

*If you want to try to escape by hitting Boris on the head with the jug, turn to page 52.*

*If you decide to wait and try to escape through the trapdoor, turn to page 53.*

You turn right and start to run. Every few steps there is another choice of turns to make. You become more and more confused until you finally come to a dead end.

A hand suddenly grips your shoulder.

"You will make a fine servant," Boris says. "Shall we return now and get some sleep?"

As you walk with him back to the shack, you wonder if Boris will be a kind master.

He answers your question when he says, "This will not happen again. From now on, you will be kept in chains. You will not be given another chance to escape."

You hope he is wrong.

**The End**

You continue to run, even though you do not know where you are going.

Suddenly you come to a dead end.

You are about to give up when you notice that the ground beneath your feet is very hard. It is not grassy like the rest of the maze.

Stooping over, you discover a trapdoor that leads into a long, dark tunnel. At the end of the tunnel is another door. You open the door carefully and peek into a room.

*Turn to page 54.*

You feel you have no choice except to help the person who is screaming. You rush through the door.

There, in the middle of the room, is a boy trapped in a net.

Using your pocketknife, you begin to cut him free.

"Don't release me," he pleads. "If they find that I have escaped, there's no telling what they will do. Please go away."

*If you decide to go away, turn to page 36.*

*If you decide to help the boy anyway, turn to page 55.*

You are frightened and start to run. You do not know where you are going and do not care. You only want to get away from this awful place.

In your panic you burst through the first door you see, hoping it will lead you out of this nightmare.

*Turn to page 57.*

You lie quietly on the cold stone floor, drifting in and out of sleep.

It is so dark that you cannot see the spider crawling toward you. You do not know that you have broken her web and that she is angry. Nor do you feel the bite of the poisonous black widow.

You finally figure out that you have been bitten by a spider when your hand begins to swell.

But by then it is too late.

**The End**

You inch your way along the cold floor toward a door that you can barely make out in the murky darkness.

Reaching up, you grab the knob and turn it slowly. Then you push it open.

You hear scraping noises on the stone floor, then strange squealing sounds. Your skin crawls as you realize that the room is filled with a squirming mass of writhing rats.

You see a door across the room. It seems to be the only way out.

*If you can gather courage to crawl through the rats to the door on the other side, turn to page 58.*

*If you want to explore further and try to find another way out, turn to page 59.*

You inch along the tunnel until you come to the end. There is a pale light shining into the darkness from a tiny window far above your head.

You are not aware that you have walked into a dungeon until you see a skeleton on the floor. The skeleton is still in chains.

You turn away. But the iron door to the dungeon falls from above and crashes closed.

You are trapped.

There is no way out.

**The End**

You do not know how far you have traveled and are beginning to think there is no end to the tunnel in this direction.

But then you come to a ladder and begin to climb. There is a trapdoor at the top, and you push it up slowly.

The first thing you notice is the smell of soup. You are in a run-down shack.

Suddenly a huge brown mastiff appears. He growls at you and bares his teeth.

*If you want to try to run past the dog and out of the shack, turn to page 60.*

*If you decide to try to make friends with the dog, turn to page 62.*

You enter the lab and are greeted by a man and a woman dressed in white coats.

"Welcome," the man says. "You look like you are a weary traveler."

"I am weary and lost and hungry," you reply.

"Don't worry about a thing," he says. "We can take care of all your needs."

"What kind of lab is this, anyway?" you ask.

"Oh, mostly we do experiments in bio-regeneration," answers the woman.

"What is bio-regeneration?" you ask.

"Oh, don't think about that now. You said you are hungry and tired. Would you like to rest here? Or would you like to go to the Throne Room and have something to eat before you sleep?"

If you want to go to the Throne Room, turn to page 64.

If you want to rest in the lab, turn to page 65.

You feel rather foolish, but you say to the dove, "All right. I'll go with you."

The dove leads you into a room in the castle where there is a group of people chained to the wall.

"Greetings," says a man. "My name is Dr. Strong. We are very happy to see you."

"Why?" you ask, suddenly afraid.

"Because in six hours we are all going to die," he explains sadly. "There are two crazed scientists in the castle who are turning people into plants and animals."

You think about the dove and realize it must have been an animal-person.

Dr. Strong continues. "The people in this room have such strong personalities that the scientists cannot turn them into animals. That is why we are going to die."

"I will help you if I can," you say.

"If you can steal the key to our chains," says Dr. Strong, "we will be able to escape."

*Turn to page 72.*

You have decided that there is nothing that could make you stay in that room one more minute. You run out the door and down the hall.

Running as fast as you can, you suddenly stop when you hear a scream. It is coming through a door that is right next to where you are standing.

*If you decide to investigate the scream, turn to page 35.*

*If you decide to go to the door at the end of the hall, turn to page 66.*

"What is going on?" you ask the man. "Why are all these animals here?"

"We are exploring life exchanges," says the man.

"What do you mean?" you ask, already afraid to hear the answer.

"Well," says the woman, "we can make a plant become an animal or make an animal become a person. And, of course, we can make a person become a plant or an animal. It is all in the computer."

*(continued on page 45)*

You are horrified by these dreadful experiments. Obviously these are very powerful people, but you are certainly sorry that you have met them.

*If you run to the door, turn to page 67.*

*If you decide to stay and cooperate with whatever they have in mind for you, turn to page 68.*

You dash through the doorway and into the hall before Boris can grab you.

You run as fast as you can down the long, empty corridors. Turning corner after corner, you finally come to a stairway.

*If you go up the stairs, turn to page 105.*

*If you go down the stairs, turn to page 107.*

"That was a wise decision," says Boris. He points to a chair in the middle of the room. "Please sit down."

You sit in the chair. The flashing lights make your skin turn strange colors. Slowly, slowly, you feel yourself drifting away.

The lights swirl around you. Soon you have the sensation that you are no longer yourself. Boris has incorporated you into his mind.

*Turn to page 69.*

Even though you know your chance of escaping is slim, you have decided to take the risk.

You run out the door as Boris unchains the dog.

*If I can only make it to the woods*, you think, *perhaps I can climb a tree.*

You feel the dog gaining on you. He is almost right behind you. Running faster now, blind with panic, you trip over a fallen branch and tumble to the ground.

When you look up, the dog is standing over you. His breath is hot and fetid.

You are trapped.

**The End**

You try to trick Boris by thinking lies. If he is going to read your mind, let him read what *you* want him to read.

*I am trapped. There's no use trying to escape,* you think.

Your trick works.

"I know you are not planning to escape," says Boris, "so I am going to take care of some business in the castle. But just in case you change your mind," he says with a wicked smile, "I'm going to unchain Killer. He will see that you don't go anywhere."

When Boris leaves, you start to feed Killer. You continue to feed him until he falls asleep.

You are finally ready to escape when your foot kicks a small metal ring on the floor and you discover a trapdoor.

*If you go through the trapdoor, turn to page 70.*

*If you leave the shack through the front door, turn to page 71.*

You stand up as quietly as you can and tiptoe to the door.

You open it. The hinges creak. The dog's ears move, but he does not wake up. You look at Boris. He is still fast asleep.

Once you are out the door, you begin to run. After a few minutes you look back toward the shack. There is no movement, and you know you are safe.

Once you are home, you wonder if your friends will believe your story.

You know one thing for sure: you are not going to take them on a tour to prove it.

**The End**

Grabbing the jug firmly by the handle, you swing it toward Boris and smack him on the side of the head. He falls unconscious to the floor.

The dog is barking wildly, and you are thankful that he is chained to the wall.

If you choose to go home now, you may stop here. You have done a good job and deserve to arrive home safely.

**The End**

*If you feel that you cannot go home until you have investigated the castle, return to the moat on page 4.*

"Have some hot chocolate before you go to sleep," says Boris, handing you a cup.

You are afraid that the drink has been drugged, so you dump the contents of the cup into the dog's bowl when Boris is not looking.

The dog drinks the hot chocolate and falls asleep immediately.

You pretend that you are sleeping.

After Boris has fallen asleep, you creep through the trapdoor. It leads into a tunnel.

You feel your way along the tunnel walls until you come to a place where there is a ladder. Climbing up, you open a door over your head and step outside.

You discover that you are in front of the castle. There is a light coming from a second-floor window.

*Turn to page 24.*

There are five people in the room, and they are all chained to the wall. You decide to go in.

"Well, look what we have here," says a man. "My name is Dr. Strong. Did you resist, too?"

"Resist what?" you ask.

"Resist the machines, of course."

"What machines?"

"You mean you don't know about the mad scientists in the lab down the hall? They turn humans into plants and animals. But we five resisted their machines because we have very strong wills. They are planning to kill us at dawn, only six hours from now. Will you help us escape?" he asks.

"Yes—if I can," you answer.

"Then you must steal the key to our chains," says Dr. Strong. "Or, if you prefer, you can go out through the tunnel, hike into town and bring back the police."

*If you choose to steal the key, turn to page 72.*

*If you choose to get the police, turn to page 73.*

After you set the boy free, he tells you that the only way out is through a secret tunnel. "But to get there," he says, "we must pass the lab. If we are caught by the scientists, we could be in real danger."

You tell the boy to go first and, if he makes it, to get out as fast as he can.

You watch as he creeps safely past the lab and into the tunnel through a trapdoor. You are pleased that he will be safe.

As you creep past the lab, you look inside.

*If you continue past the lab and into the tunnel, turn to page 70.*

*If you are so curious about the lab that you must find out what is going on in there, turn to page 41.*

You find yourself in a wondrous room filled with people. There is gold and silver and crystal everywhere.

"What is this place?" you ask a friendly-looking man.

"It is the Throne Room," he answers. "The best place I have ever been." Then he adds, "Except, of course, when the selection is made."

You ask what he means by that.

"Every day one of us is chosen to go with the scientists," he explains. "And the chosen ones never return. Other than that, life here is a continual delight."

You wonder how life can be a delight when you might disappear the next day.

"Please," says the man, pointing to a banquet table, "have something to eat."

*If you decide to eat, turn to page 76.*

*If you suspect that the food might be poisoned, turn to page 77.*

You begin to make your way slowly toward the door. The rats are everywhere, but you are amazed to discover that they do not touch you.

You reach the door on the other side of the room, thinking all the time that these are not ordinary rats. You open the door and discover that you have found the way out of the castle.

You feel strangely grateful to the rats. Without thinking, you bend over and touch one in silent thanks.

With that gesture, something extraordinary happens.

*Turn to page 78.*

The rats disgust you. You close the door. But not before some of them escape.

You are weak and try to get away from them as you crawl on the cold, slimy floor. But it is too late. You cannot move.

You feel the rats crawling all over you. This is

**The End**

The dog is as surprised as you are at your decision. He jumps back. Without hesitating, you spring out from the tunnel and run across the room.

You are out the door in an instant, and you slam it behind you.

You hear a roar overhead and look up. There is a helicopter flying over the trees. You take off your jacket and wave it.

The helicopter hovers over you for a minute, before it begins to descend. You are relieved. You know that you will soon be home.

*(continued on page 61)*

You have done a great job. If you wish, you may stop here.

**The End**

*If you would like to explore the castle, signal to the helicopter that you are safe and then go back to the beam of light you saw earlier on page 9.*

You emerge from the tunnel very slowly so that you do not startle the dog. All the time you talk to it in a soothing voice.

Just as you have begun to feel comfortable with the dog, the front door opens and a scruffy, bearded man enters.

"Corner the intruder, Killer," the man commands the dog.

*(continued on page 63)*

In no time, you are taken to a room in the castle tower.

There is nothing in the room except a bed.

*If you decide to tie the bed sheets together and make a rope so that you can lower yourself out the window and into the moat, turn to page 79.*

*If you decide to wait and see if you can discover a less dangerous way out, turn to page 80.*

The scientists take you to the most elegant room you have ever seen. The chandelier is made of sparkling crystal. The walls are paneled with gold. There are velvet couches and deep, soft chairs, and people resting and eating. You nod to them politely.

Once you have finished your meal, you realize that a change has taken place in you. You are no longer curious about what is happening here. The food has taken away your curiosity.

*Turn to page 81.*

You are so exhausted that you are no longer hungry. You are grateful to the two scientists when they show you a soft, warm bed. You can think of nothing better than a good night's sleep.

When you wake up in the morning, you are horrified to see that your body is now small and furry, and that you have grown a long bushy tail. You have a craving for acorns.

Suddenly you understand the full meaning of bio-regeneration.

**The End**

You go through the door and discover that you are in an ordinary living room. As you decide to sit down, a big yellow chair slides across the floor to where you are standing. You feel a breeze but see nobody.

Then a glass of orange juice floats across the room toward you. Again you feel a breeze.

You are frightened and want to run, but you are fascinated by the fact that there might be a ghost in the room with you.

Even though you are thirsty, you are afraid to drink the juice.

*If you leave and go up the stairs at the far end of the room, turn to page 21.*

*If you stay, turn to page 82.*

You run past the two scientists toward the door.

The scientists make no effort to catch you, but you discover that you are being followed by a beam of light.

You run through the door and down the hall. You zigzag back and forth, trying to avoid the beam. But you cannot escape it. You feel the heat of the light piercing your body. You feel a tingle. Then you are horrified as you watch your body disappear.

You have been transformed into a ghost.

*If you try to find other ghosts in the castle, turn to page 83.*

*If you go back to the lab to try to find a solution to your problem, turn to page 85.*

You're very frightened, but you know that there is no way you can outwit these scientists. After all, hadn't they just made you disappear and reappear?

"You needn't be afraid," the woman says to you. "We won't hurt you. Just stand in this glass booth and you can become one of our family."

Relieved that they will not hurt you, you move into the booth. You watch the scientists as they pull levers, push buttons and set some dials. There is a high, pulsating sound in the booth.

You try to scream when you see that your feet are turning into roots, but there is nothing you can do.

You have been turned into a banana tree.

**The End**

It is an hour later. You are still in the room with Boris. You belong to him now, but you do not care.

*This is where I belong,* you think, a smile creeping over your face. *This is what I should be doing. It is pleasant and warm in the castle with Boris. He is a nice man after all. I think I will like it here. . . .*

**The End**

Opening the trapdoor, you descend into the tunnel. It is dark and cold and slippery inside. You move along slowly until you come to a fork.

*If you go to the left, turn to page 38.*

*If you go to the right, turn to page 94.*

You slip quietly past the sleeping dog. Once outside, you start to jog in the direction of home.

You know that you will arrive home safely. You hope that you can get the police to return to the castle with you. Otherwise, everything about the castle and Boris will always remain a mystery.

**The End**

Together you work out a plan. Dr. Strong explains that at night there is only one scientist in the lab. Tonight is the man's turn, and he will come in to check the prisoners as he always does.

The plan is that just before the scientist comes in, you will hide behind the door. While he is inside, you will slip out the door and get the key from the lab.

You are scared—so scared that you are not certain you can perform the task.

"Wouldn't it be better," you ask, "if I were to use my Swiss Army knife to try to file through the chains?"

"The choice is yours," says Dr. Strong. "I cannot force you to risk your life."

*If you decide to try to steal the key, turn to page 101.*

*If you decide to stay and file through the chains, turn to page 102.*

"The escape plan is this," says Dr. Strong. "If you go back through the tunnel and stay to your right, you will come out in the woods. The path to town is well marked, so you won't get lost. But do remember to hurry; our time is short."

It is more than ten miles back to town. You know that in less than six hours, Dr. Strong and his friends will be killed.

*If you walk back to town in order to save your strength, turn to page 103.*

*If you run back to town in order to save time, turn to page 104.*

The tone of her voice seems gentle, but the words seem threatening. You are confused.

"Do you help lost people find their way home?" you ask.

"Oh, no. I make you comfortable right here. There is no need for you to go home ever again."

At that moment the vine above you reaches down and curls around your body. You try to twist yourself free, but the more you struggle, the more entangled you become.

*(continued on page 75)*

"I will release you if you come with me to the lab," says the woman. "If you refuse to come, I will leave you here alone with the vines."

*If you decide to go to the lab, turn to page 112.*

*If you decide to stay alone with the vines, turn to page 114.*

Everything you eat is delicious. And the people in the room are as wonderful as the food. You cannot ever remember being so happy.

The bed you sleep on that night is made of the softest down feathers.

When you awaken in the morning, the scientist is in the room. He has come to make the selection.

Unfortunately, *you* are chosen.

**The End**

Despite the fact that you are ravenous from lack of food, you refuse to eat.

You suspect that the people have been drugged by something in the food. Otherwise, why would they go so willingly with the scientists?

You announce to the people that the food is dangerous and that you are going to throw it out the window.

They just stand around smiling as the food drops into the moat, and you know for certain that they are drugged.

By early morning the effect of the drugs has worn off. Suddenly the people are angry that they are being kept here against their will.

You are proclaimed a hero, and together you formulate a plan to capture the scientists when they enter the room.

Soon you will all be free and safe.

**The End**

Before your eyes, the rats begin to change into people.

Your courage has been rewarded. The rats were victims of some evil experiments that had been taking place in the castle. You have broken the spell.

With a loud cheer of thanks, the newly liberated people tell you that they will now lead you to safety.

### The End

*If your curiosity will not allow you to leave until you find out what is going on in this strange place, say good-bye to the people and go back to the shack on page 7.*

You carefully take the sheets and tear them into strips. Then you tie the pieces together to form one long rope.

After securing the rope to the bed, you lower yourself out the window.

Below you is the moat. But the rope does not reach that far, and you are forced to drop the last twenty feet into the water.

Just as you let go, you see a shark's fin cutting through the water. You make a huge splash and swim as quickly as you can, scrambling onto dry land just in time.

You are safe. Your courage has been rewarded. Soon you will be home.

**The End**

You wait several days in the tower, hoping that someone will come to release you. You have had nothing to eat and are ravenously hungry. Soon the hunger passes, but you are very weak.

You decide that you will make a sheet rope and go out the window. You make the rope and lower yourself into the moat below.

But you are so weak from lack of food that you drop into the water. You are too tired to notice the shark's fin that is moving your way.

**The End**

A man and a woman come over to you.

"Something has happened to my mind," you say.

"Ah, yes," the man says with a smile. "It has happened to all of us in the Throne Room. We are content. The food is wonderful. The chairs and pillows are the softest in the world. We all plan to stay here forever. After all, why would we want to leave?"

"We leave only when we are called," says the woman happily.

"Called?" you ask.

"Ah, yes," says the man. "Each day one of us is called and taken away. Those who go never return."

You realize then, to your horror, that you and everyone else in the room have been drugged by something that has taken away not only your curiosity but also your will. You know that you will never escape. You don't even care.

**The End**

You say, "No thank you," to the glass that is suspended in midair in front of you.

The glass then moves to a table and sits itself down.

On the table is a piece of paper and a pen. The pen moves and writes: You must escape now or you will be turned into a ghost like me. Follow the path to the right of the bridge and you will come to a town.

You are stunned. You decide that you must do what the ghostly hand says.

*Turn to page 96.*

You float down the hall and come to a door. You decide to go in. After all, nobody will see you now.

You are in a living room. There is another ghost sitting at a table.

"What has happened to us?" you ask, grateful that you can see her.

"Can't you look at yourself and answer that

*(continued on page 84)*

question?" the ghost replies. "We are trapped in the other world. You must accept your fate. So come. Sit down and eat with me. Then we can play a game of Monopoly."

*If you decide to accept your fate and play Monopoly, turn to page 97.*

*If you decide to fight your fate and not give up, turn to page 98.*

When the two scientists go on their nightly rounds, you enter the lab and begin to pull levers and flip switches on the giant computer. Nothing works.

Just as you are about to give up, you discover a lever that says DANGER—DO NOT TOUCH.

*If you pull the lever, turn to page 99.*

*If you decide not to pull the lever, turn to page 100.*

You open the door carefully, fearful of what you might find inside.

Suddenly you are swept into the room by a huge hairy arm. You try to scream, but no sound comes out.

You look up into the scarred face of an eight-foot monster. His eyes are blood red; his teeth are brown and jagged; his foul smell makes you gag.

In a deep, growling voice he demands, "What are you doing here?"

If you run toward the door, turn to page 88.

If you decide to answer his question, turn to page 89.

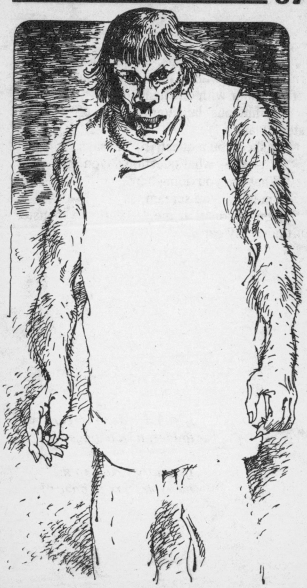

You take two steps, and suddenly you are running in the air. The monster has lifted you off the floor with one hand.

His hideous laughter echoes off the cold stone walls.

"I asked you a question," he says.

"Wh—wh—what question?" you ask.

"What are you doing here?"

"I'm lost," you scream.

"Don't scream at me," orders the monster. "It hurts my ears."

*If you decide to scream even louder, turn to page 90.*

*If you try to talk to the monster, turn to page 91.*

"I heard the pounding on the door," you answer, "and I thought someone was in trouble."

"You are absolutely correct," says the monster, scratching the greasy hair on his chest. "Someone *is* in trouble."

The monster's bloody eyes glare at you. Pointing to two doors on the other side of the room, he says, "One of those doors opens into a room full of hungry rattlesnakes. The other leads to a tunnel. Choose one and get out of here."

Shaking, you open the door on the right. It is dark and silent, and you realize that fortunately you have chosen the tunnel.

*Turn to page 23.*

The monster is holding you in midair, close to his face.

You take a deep breath, open your mouth wide and scream so loudly in his ear that your stomach hurts.

"No, no, no!" shrieks the monster, dropping you to the floor as he covers his ears. "Stop screaming! I can't stand it!"

You scream even louder. The monster falls to the floor, writhing in pain. Reaching out, he grabs your arm.

"If you do not stop, I will tear your arm off!" he manages to say.

*If you stop screaming, turn to page 92.*

*If you try to scream one more time, turn to page 93.*

"I'm sorry," you say. "I didn't mean to hurt you."

"Good," says the monster. "Now it's time for dinner."

He hands you a plate covered with slimy, wriggling worms.

"Eat," he orders.

You want to vomit. "I can't," you say.

"It's easy," he replies as he picks up a handful of worms and pops them one by one into his drooling mouth.

"Eat," he says again. "Or be eaten."

He hands you a fat, slimy worm. You stare at it, but you cannot eat it.

The monster reaches down to your plate and grabs all the worms in his hand. Then he finishes every one of them, licking his oozing lips when he is finished.

"A fine appetizer. Now for the main course," he says, reaching out and grabbing you.

**The End**

The room is silent. The monster rises.

"Now you have made me angry," he growls.

Reaching out, he grabs you around your waist and begins to swing you back and forth.

Finally he flings you through an open window. You feel yourself falling. You look down and see the moat beneath you. You splash into the water and swim as fast as you can to the other shore. You know that you will find your way home eventually.

**The End**

You open your mouth to scream, but the only sound that escapes is a hoarse squeak. You have lost your voice.

The monster stands up.

"Nobody screams at me like that," he says.

"I'm sorry," you reply, really frightened now.

"It's too late to be sorry," says the monster, as he moves toward you. "The damage is already done. You will never scream again."

**The End**

You move carefully down the right fork of the tunnel. The path is damp and slimy. Furry things keep running over your feet. Finally your hand touches a ladder. You do not know where it leads, but you think that anywhere is better than this place.

You climb out and find yourself in a cemetery. You see a light in a second-floor window of the castle. In order to reach it, you will have to walk among the tombstones.

*If you decide to go back into the tunnel and look for another exit, turn to page 23.*

*If you choose to go to the light in the castle, turn to page 24.*

You walk for several hours before you finally come to a town.

When you tell the police about the ghost, they laugh at you. They simply cannot believe such a preposterous story. You nod sadly and ask them to take you home.

**The End**

You have just put hotels on Boardwalk and Park Place. You are enjoying the game. You have given up fighting and have accepted your fate.

You will always be a ghost.

**The End**

You refuse to believe that you must go on being a ghost forever.

You float away from the living room, thinking that the strange beam of light might be the answer—if it changed you one way, it might change you again.

You finally find the light beam outside the castle and hurry to stand in it.

Very slowly your old body begins to take on its former shape. You are joyous and hope that the other ghost is watching. But you fear that she has given up.

Once you are yourself again, you hurry into the woods. It takes you three days to find your way home. You are exhausted and hungry. But you are safe at last.

**The End**

You reach over slowly and put your hand on the lever. You hesitate. Then you take a deep breath and pull.

Gradually, the computer turns a pale pink, then bright red.

You move to the doorway just as the computer explodes.

When the dust settles, you are amazed to discover that all the plants and animals in the room have turned back into people. You, too, are once more yourself.

"You are a hero!" the people shout.

You know that there are enough of you to overpower the scientists when they reenter the room. Then you and all your new friends will have a fabulous celebration.

**The End**

Since you do not want to risk the possible consequences of pulling the lever, stop here. You will remain a ghost, but you will always be happy and in no danger.

**The End**

*If, however, you change your mind and decide that you want to pull the lever, turn to page 99.*

You hear the footsteps of the scientist as he walks toward the room. You step quietly behind the door just before he enters.

Once he is inside, you slip out and run into the lab.

You grab the key, run out and hide in a doorway until the scientist returns to the lab.

Then, to the whispered cheers of your new friends, you unlock their chains.

You all know that the next time the scientist enters the room, you can overpower him, then catch his partner. Then you will free all the inhabitants of this mysterious castle.

Many people will owe their lives to you.

You are a hero!

**The End**

You take your Swiss Army knife out of your pocket and begin to file Dr. Strong's chain.

You finish just as the scientist opens the door.

Before you can run, the scientist grabs you and chains you to the wall, next to Dr. Strong.

"You, too, will die at dawn," the scientist says.

When he leaves the room, you discover that Dr. Strong is free.

Later that night he is able to sneak into the lab and steal the key.

Soon you are all free.

**The End**

You walk briskly and steadily. Every hour you stop and rest for five minutes. You are amazed at how quickly you reach your destination.

When the police hear your story, they immediately set out to save Dr. Strong and his friends. There is plenty of time.

You are rightfully proud of yourself. You have performed bravely.

**The End**

You start to run. You are young and strong, capable of running a very long distance before tiring.

But after six miles of running, you cannot go on. You are exhausted, and you must rest.

You fall into a deep sleep and stay there for a much longer time than you intended. By the time you reach the police, there is only an hour left.

But the police move quickly. Within minutes they fly off in a helicopter. You hope they will arrive before it is too late.

**The End**

The stairs circle around and around. All the time you wonder where they could be taking you.

The top of the stairs leads directly to a door. You open it and step inside with relief.

There, to your horror, is Boris, gently rocking back and forth in his chair.

"What took you so long?" he asks with a sinister smile.

"How did you know?" you ask.

*(continued on page 106)*

"It was easy," says Boris. "Every turn you made was determined by me. As I told you, the power of the mind is my business."

*If you decide there is no choice but to stay with Boris, turn to page 108.*

*If you want to risk your life and jump out the window into the moat below, turn to page 109.*

You run as fast as you can down the stairs,
never stopping until you reach the bottom. You
listen for Boris's footsteps, but there are none.

You have escaped.

The problem is that you do not know where
you are or where to go now.

On either side of you, there is a door.

*If you open the door on your
right, turn to page 54.*

*If you open the door on your
left, turn to page 111.*

"Will you teach me how to expand the powers of my mind?" you ask, trying to stall long enough to think of a way out.

"Do you think I am a fool?" asks Boris. "I'll never give up my power."

You turn to look at the door. But it slams closed and bolts itself.

"That's another one of my talents," Boris says.

You realize that you are helpless. There is nothing you can do. There is no place you can go.

You belong to Boris now.

**The End**

You would rather risk your life than be forever controlled by Boris.

You leap through the window.

*(continued on page 110)*

Hitting the water feet first, you sink quickly to the bottom of the moat. When your feet touch bottom, you bend your knees and push yourself back up to the surface.

Gasping for breath, you swim to the side of the moat and climb out.

You run into the woods, knowing that sooner or later you will find your way home.

**The End**

Once inside, you discover you are in a beautiful garden room.

You stretch out on a lounge chair, surrounded by lush plants and vines. You are so exhausted that you close your eyes and drift off to sleep.

An hour later you are awakened by the soft voice of a woman in a white coat.

"Are you all right?" she asks with a smile.

"I think so," you answer.

"What happened?" she asks.

"I just escaped from a man named Boris, and now I am lost."

"Good," she says. "I will take care of you. I've had lots of experience dealing with lost people. I know exactly what has to be done."

*Turn to page 74.*

You are being crushed by the vine, and you tell the woman that you will go with her.

The lab is filled with more plants. There are caged animals everywhere, and you do not know what to think.

*(continued on page 113)*

"What kind of lab is this?" you ask.
"A bio-regeneration lab," she answers.
"What is that?"
"Life exchanges," she answers.
You do not like the sound of that at all.

*If you try to run out the door and escape, turn to page 36.*

*If you are curious about the experiments and want to stay in the lab, turn to page 115.*

You watch the woman walk out the door.

Very slowly you move your hand to your pocket and reach inside. You grip your knife, pull it out and carefully open the blade.

In no time you cut yourself free.

You grab the vine by its longest branch and move to the window. You feel the vine twisting, trying to get away. But you keep your grip and crawl through the window.

The weight of your body forces the vine to unwind slowly, and you are lowered gently to the ground.

You are at the edge of the moat. You dive in and swim across. Then you climb out quickly and run into the woods.

You know that if you can escape Boris and the threat of the vines, you are strong enough and smart enough to find your way home.

**The End**

"What do you mean by life exchanges?" you ask.

"We change one form of life into another. For instance, that plant used to be a deer."

"Do you also change people into other forms of life?" you ask fearfully.

"Oh, yes. That is our specialty. That is what we do with lost people. Many have found their way here. But few have ever left."

You are terrified now and look around for some way to save yourself.

You look at the giant computer that covers one entire wall. At the far corner of the computer is a red lever that is marked DANGER— DO NOT TOUCH.

"Come," says the woman as she opens the door of an empty cage. "Get in."

*Turn to page 116.*

You panic. You know that if you get in the cage, you will not come out as yourself.

You do not know what will happen if you pull the lever, but you are willing to gamble. You have nothing left to lose.

With a burst of energy you dash to the lever and pull it down hard.

In a series of small explosions, the computer crumbles.

"My work!" the woman screams. "You have destroyed years of experiments and scientific study."

As you look around the room, you watch the plants and animals gradually turning back into their original forms. You have released them all from their entrapment.

There is nothing that the scientist can do now. You are all free.

**The End**

# NOW THAT YOU'VE COME TO THE END OF YOUR VERY OWN ADVENTURE DO YOU KNOW

## WHICH WAY

## TO GO FOR MORE?

Well, just try any or all of these thrilling, chilling
adventure-on-every-page **WHICH WAY** ™ books!

# KIDS LOVE ANIMALS!

And you will love all these exciting, wonderful stories about dogs, cats, raccoons, and horses.

**BAMBI by Felix Salten** 46138/$2.95
"Beauty, grace, and individuality rare among works of fiction."
—*Saturday Review*

**SCRUFFY by Jack Stoneley** 41096/$1.95
"Scruffy is the 'Oliver Twist' of dogs. She's a gutsy orphan who'll capture your heart. The story is a delight!"
—*Mordecai Siegal, author of The Good Dog Book*

**THE HOUSE OF THIRTY CATS
by Mary Calhoun** 42064/$1.95
"This is a delightfully 'catty' story with a strong appeal."
—*Denver Post*

**FROSTY: A RACCOON TO REMEMBER
by Harriett E. Weaver** 42094/$1.95
"It is impossible to read this winning story without sharing the author's affection for the raccoon . . ."
—*Publishers Weekly*

**BIG MUTT by John Reese** 43921/$2.25
"Set in the sheep-raising country of North Dakota . . . it successfully combines a moving dog story with exciting adventure."
—*The New York Times*

**"NATIONAL VELVET" by Enid Bagnold**
46528/$2.50
". . . pure enchantment, excitement and enjoyment."
—*The New York Times*

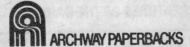 **ARCHWAY PAPERBACKS**

332